WEiRDO 4

SUPER WEIRD!

Scholastic Press
345 Pacific Highway Lindfield NSW 2070
An imprint of Scholastic Australia Pty Limited (ABN 11 000 614 577)
PO Box 579 Gosford NSW 2250
www.scholastic.com.au

Part of the Scholastic Group
Sydney • Auckland • New York • Toronto • London • Mexico City
• New Delhi • Hong Kong • Buenos Aires • Puerto Rico

First published by Scholastic Australia in 2015.
Text copyright © Anh Do, 2015.
Illustrations copyright © Jules Faber, 2015.

National Library of Australia Cataloguing-in-Publication entry
Author: Do, Anh, author.
Title: Super Weird / Anh Do; illustrated by Jules Faber.
ISBN: 9781743629314 (paperback)
Series: Do, Anh. WeirDo; 4.
Target Audience: For primary school age.
Other Authors/Contributors: Faber, Jules, 1971-, illustrator.
Dewey Number: A823.4

Typeset in Grenadine MVB, Push Ups and Lunch Box.

Printed by RR Donnelley.
Scholastic Australia's policy, in association with
RR Donnelley, is to use papers that are renewable and
made efficiently from wood grown in responsibly managed
forests, so as to minimise its environmental footprint.

25 24 23   21 22 23 24 25 / 2

BLAH.
BLAH.
BLAH

ANH DO

Illustrated by JULES FABER

WEIRDO 4

SUPER WEIRD!

A SCHOLASTIC PRESS BOOK
FROM SCHOLASTIC AUSTRALIA

CHAPTER 1

You already know that me and my family are a **bit** weird!

weird

weird

weird

weird

weird

weird

super weird

also weird!

But guess what? Our new puppy FiDo is **WEIRD**, too!

FiDo's a sausage dog. He has **super short legs** and a **super loooooooong** body.

He can't jump very high, but he can **wriggle under** almost anything!

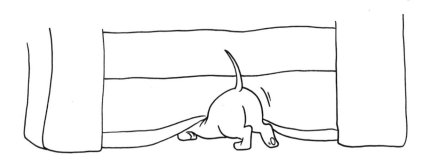

He keeps wriggling into **weird** places and finding things we haven't seen in

aaaaaaaaaaaages!

Like Sally's **socks** ...

THAT'S WHERE
MY SPOTTY
SOCK WENT!

And Dad's **gadgets** ...

YOU FOUND
MY OLD VIDEO
CAMERA!

Roger's **dummy** ...

And Granddad's **teeth**!

FiDo's **really** brave. He's not scared of anything.

He's like a **SUPER** sausage dog.

IS IT A DOG? IS IT A SAUSAGE?
NO, IT'S **SUPER** SAUSAGE DOG!

Faster than a **speeding bullfrog!**

More **powerful** than a **crazy chicken**!

Able to get under **anything** in a single crawl!

In fact, both of our pets are **really brave**. Blockhead isn't scared of anything, either. He's like the **bravest parrot** in town!

He's so brave, they should name a **bravery award** after him.

OFFICER JACKSON, FOR BRAVELY RESCUING A FAMILY FROM THEIR SINKING BOAT, I AWARD YOU . . . A GOLDEN BLOCKHEAD!

Oh, I forgot . . .

Blockhead **IS** scared of one thing.

Just **one** thing.

But that's nothing, really.

Blockhead and FiDo have become **best friends**.

They **sing** together.

They **sleep** together.

They practise **barking** together.

They even watch **funny TV shows** together.

Their **favourite** TV show is called '**Funniest Pets**'. People send in videos of their pets doing **funny things**!

11

Blockhead and **FiDo** do <u>**heaps**</u> of funny things, too. They like to get around together like this

YEEHAH!

It's <u>**SO funny**</u> watching them **ride around** like that!

12

FiDo's not very fast, 'cos of his little **legs.**
But that's kind of why I like him even more!

I'm **short** and **can't run very fast**, either!

— Perfect! —

CHAPTER 2

I guess everyone has something they are good at (even me!). And my dad is **reeeeeally good** at **SMELLING** things.

It's like he's a **superhero**, and **smelling things** is his **super power**!

NOSEMAN
to the rescue!

It would be **great** if he could
use his power to <u>fight crime!</u>

THANK YOU, **NOSEMAN!**
WITHOUT YOUR HELP, WE WOULD
NEVER HAVE CAUGHT
GARLIC-BREATH JONES!

If you talk to Dad for a bit, he can tell what you ate for breakfast!

GUESS WHAT I HAD FOR BREAKFAST?

PORRIDGE AND A BANANA!

YES!

He can even tell what **FiDo's** eaten!

Dad says it's because he has **a GREAT nose.**

He's **SO good** at smelling things that he can **smell smoke** from a **loooooooooong way away.**

He's always ready to **leap** into action as soon as he smells smoke in the air. He's had a few **false alarms**, but he always says it's

better to be
safe than sorry . . .

Like, there was this one time when we were

bushwalking

with

Granddad . . . >>>>

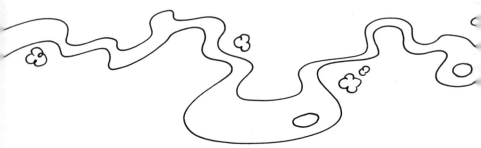

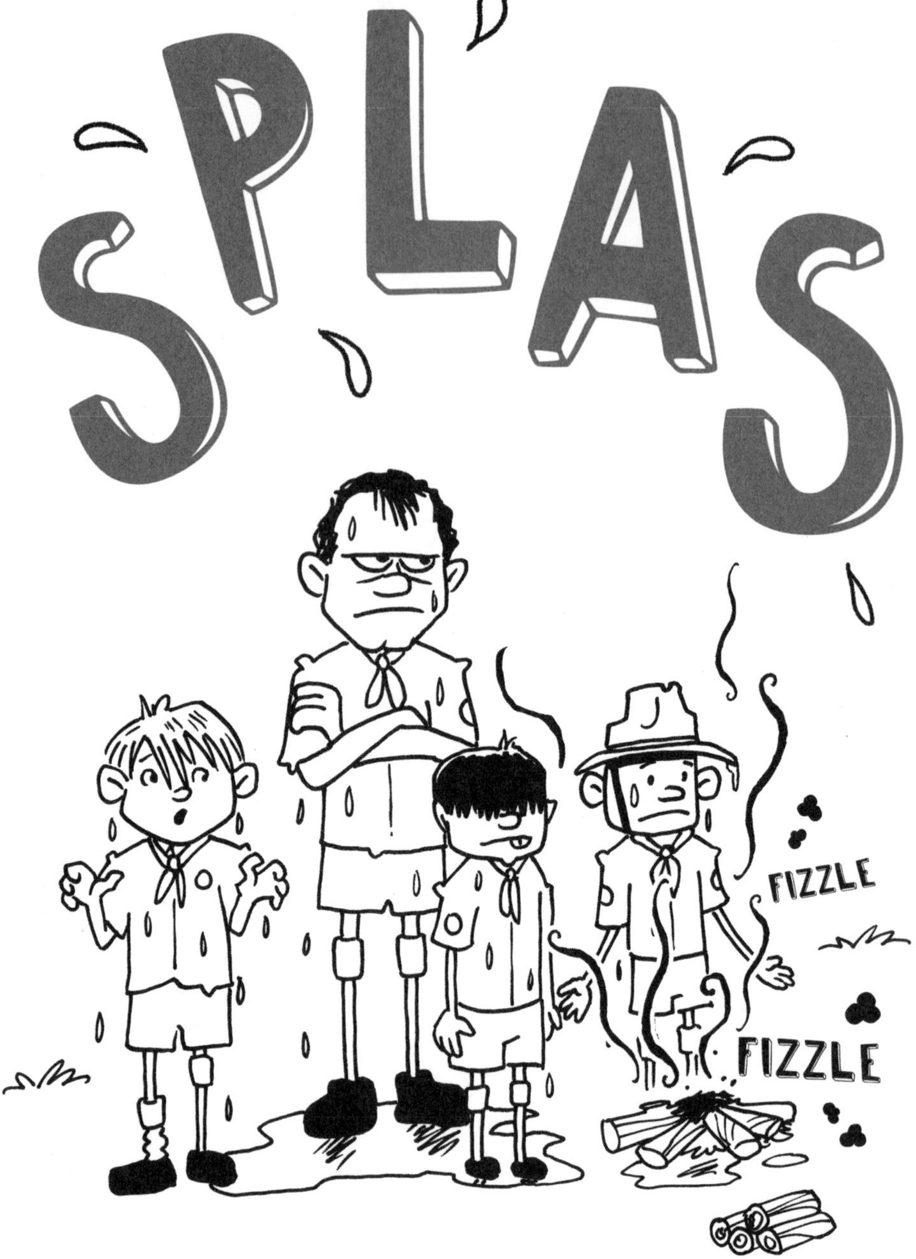
SPLASH
FIZZLE
FIZZLE

Then there was that other time when we were at the retirement village

visiting

Great

Aunty Flo . . . 》》》》

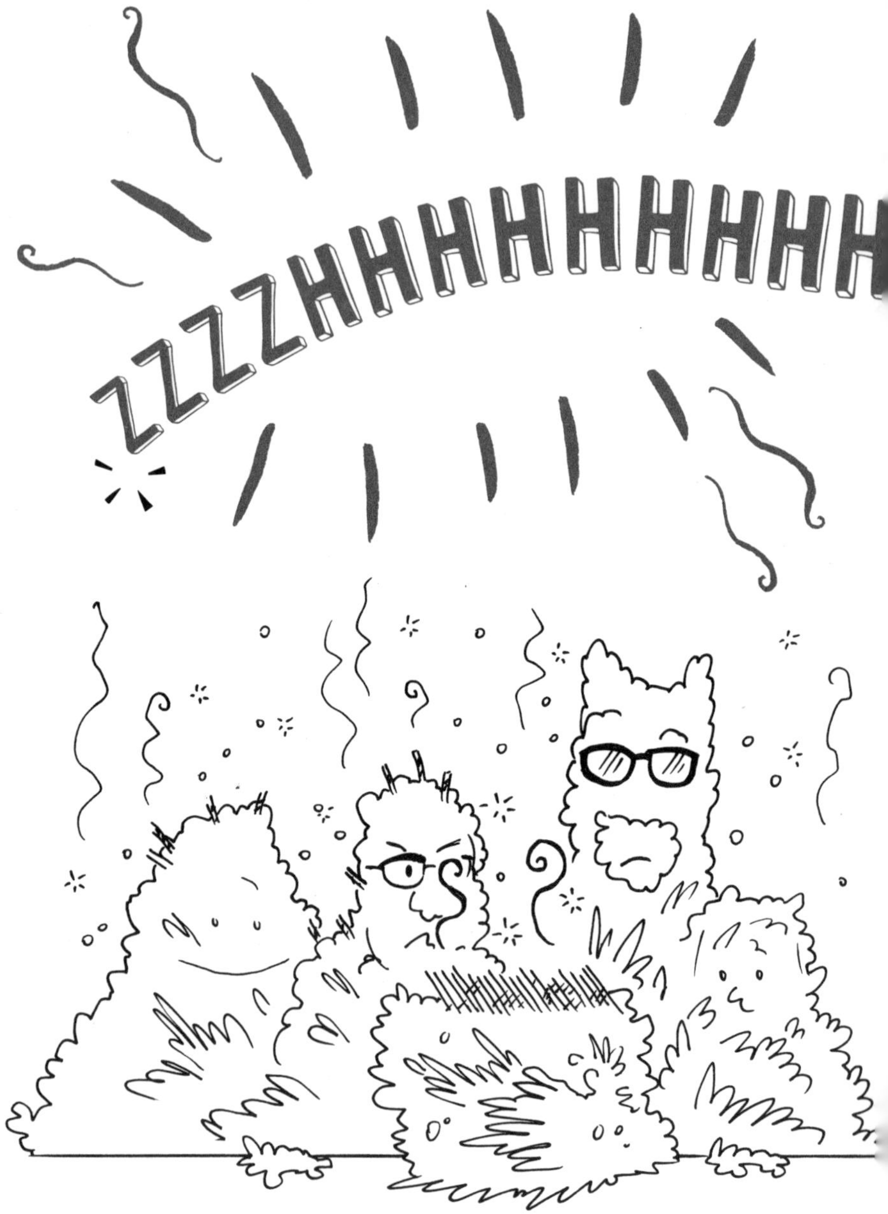
ZZZZHHHHHHHHHHHH

But when there really is an emergency,
Dad and his **great nose** will make for one

AWESOME firefighter!

That's right, my dad's training to become
a FIREFIGHTER!

I've been going to training with him on the
weekends. Just to watch. I think it would be
a <u>very</u> cool job.

Maybe when I grow up and get a bit bigger,
I can join him!

me, bigger!

We would make the **best** firefighting team!

But to become a firefighter, you have to reach a certain **height.** When they measured Dad, **he just made it!**

Lucky for Dad, he woke up that morning with **really bad bed hair.** His **EXTRA BIG** hair got him just over the line.

YOU MUST BE
THIS TALL

Bed hair is really just another way of saying

WEIRD HAIR.

My whole family sometimes wakes up with **really funny** bed hair.

Mum

Sally

Granddad

← Me

But the **WORST** of all is Roger!

ROGER! →

I often wish I was taller ... 'cos being short can be **pretty annoying**.

Last year, our family went to the **Easter Show** and I was **too short** to go on the **big** roller-coaster.

HEY KIDS! YOU MUST BE THIS TALL TO RIDE!

They let kids **heaps younger** than me on the ride, **just** because they were **taller.**

YAY!

BUT HE'S JUST A BABY!

How could they let a **giant baby** on and not me? I think the rule should be:

IF YOU'RE WEARING A NAPPY, STICK TO THE KIDDY RIDES!

Believe me, **NO-ONE** on a roller-coaster wants to sit next to someone who's able to

go to
the toilet
in their <u>own pants.</u>

And sometimes at the supermarket,
I can't reach my **favourite chips**!

They're **always** on the **top shelf!**

yuck

yuckier

worst chips,
YUCK!

TOOTHPASTE
FLAVOUR

Maybe I should JOIN THE CIRCUS and learn to walk on stilts.

But I don't know if they'd allow that at the supermarket.

CAN THE KID ON THE STILTS
PLEASE REPORT TO SECURITY
IMMEDIATELY?

the best chips

But the **biggest problem** with being short
is that it makes it hard to play lots of **sports.**

Like **basketball**...

I wish there was a game called SHORTBALL.
It'd be just like basketball, but the ring would
be close to the ground.

All the BIG GUYS would trip over
themselves trying to shoot baskets and the

LITTLE GUYS
would be the CHAMPS!

LITTLE GUYS | 00:00 | TALL GUYS
65 | | 32

Who am I kidding?

Life is

pretty tough

for small guys!

CHAPTER 3

Today, it's **PET DAY** at school! We all get to bring in our pets to show everyone.

It's **funny** how <u>so many</u> people look like their pets.

Blake

Jake

Mullet

Ferret

Jenny

Penny

Mary

Scary

Toby Hogan

Hulk Hogan

But then there are others that look
<u>nothing alike</u>.

Like Henry...

and his dog

and his pet rock

Then there's Bella...

I thought Bella would have something like a **fluffy** cat...

or a **long-eared bunny**...

or maybe a little **poodle**...

Man, was I **wrong!**

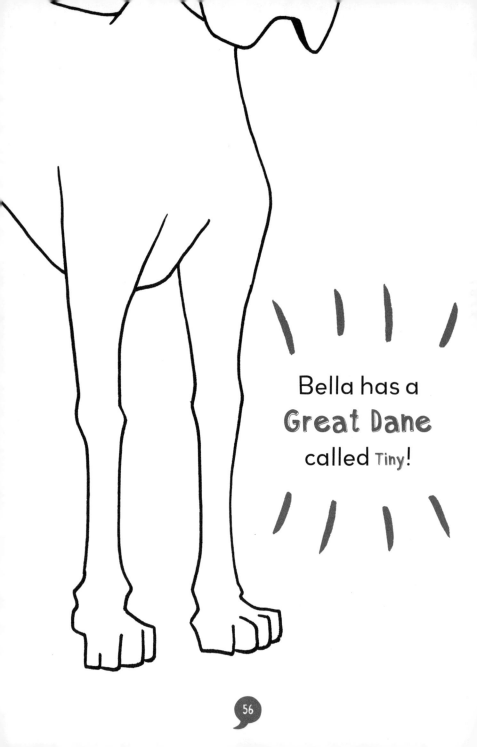

Bella has a
Great Dane
called Tiny!

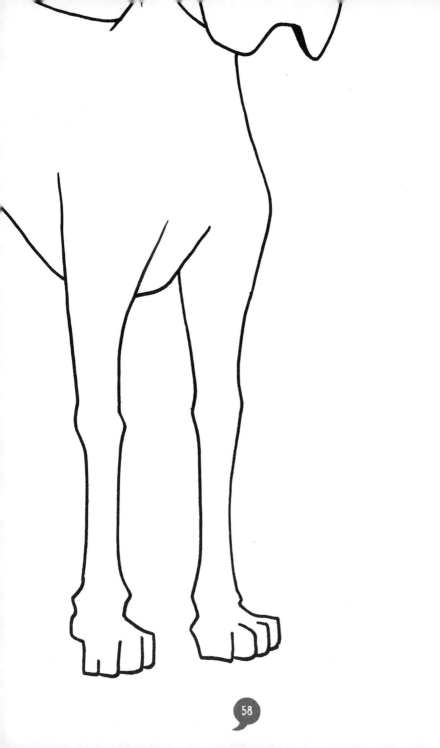

58

Tiny is **as big as a horse!**

A **really,**

really

BIG horse!

'Um, hi Tiny,' I said, walking up to him.

I'd never felt so small!

'He's friendly,' said Bella. 'Big, but friendly. Tiny,' she said to the dog, 'say hello to my friend, WeirDo.'

His bark **nearly** blew me **over**!

WOW, BELLA,
UMMM, CUTE DOG.
IS HE GOING TO RACE IN THE
MELBOURNE CUP
THIS YEAR?

Bella smiled at me and I blushed.

'He likes you,' said Bella. 'I knew he would.'

Then Tiny **licked** me!

I was knocked off my feet and landed with a

Bella helped me up.

SEE! HE REAAAAALLLY LIKES YOU!

That's funny, 'cos I **reaaaaallly** like Bella!

I showed Bella **my** pets.

'You must be FiDo,' said Bella, 'and you must be Blockhead.'

She picked up FiDo and gave him a **cuddle**. Blockhead **jumped** onto her finger and **wriggled**.

HAHAHA!

Meanwhile, Mr McDool was rounding up everyone and their pets for the

PET PARADE. 〉〉〉〉

He'd even

brought in

his own pet!

The McDrools!

Everyone lined up with their pets and, **one-by-one**, we started making our way **around the playground.**

First, Tiny **galloped** along with Bella and <u>everyone gasped.</u>

YIKES!

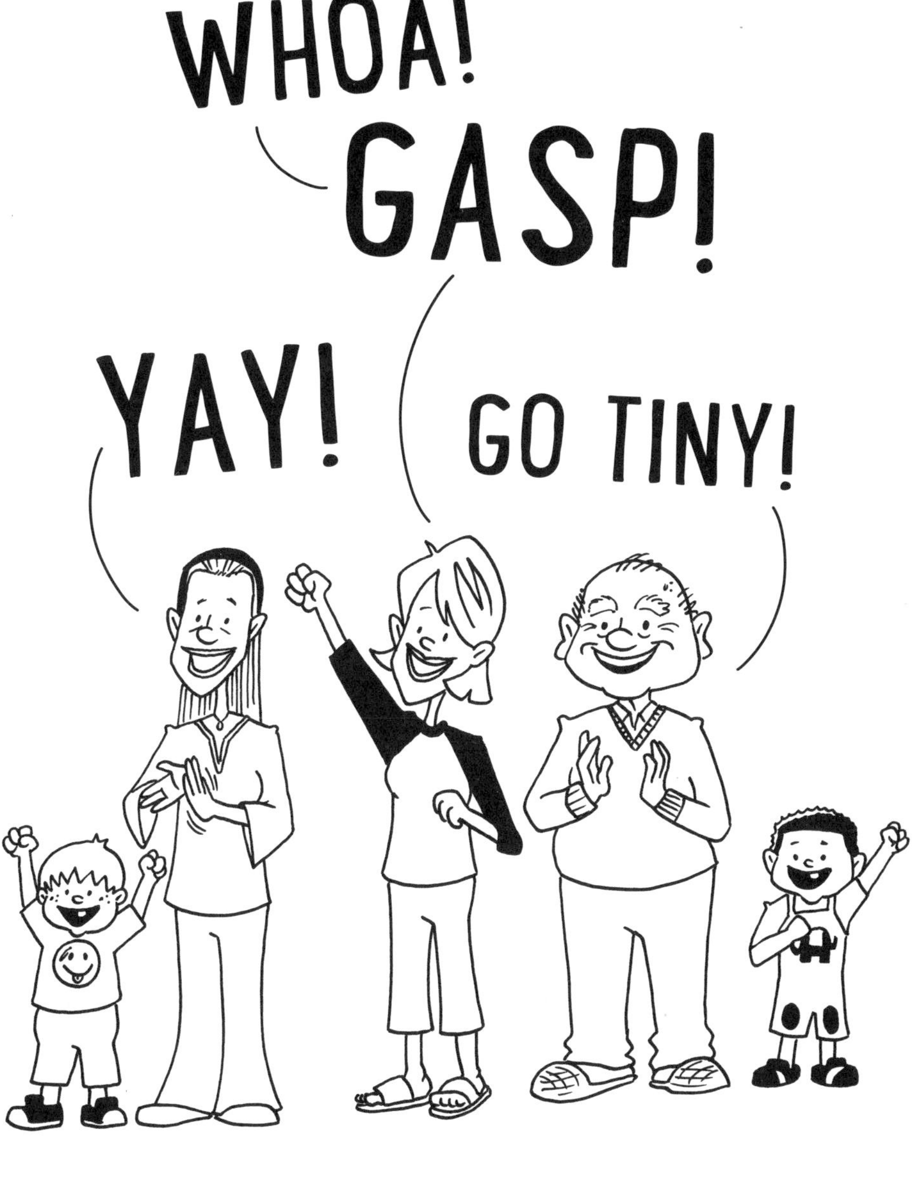
WHOA!
GASP!
YAY!
GO TINY!

Next, there was Wendy and her **rabbit** hopping backwards,

a handstanding **pig**

and a stunned **goldfish**.

Sally had given me her old **toy pony's saddle** to put on FiDo and a **cowboy hat** to put on Blockhead.

When they ran out with me—

Blockhead riding on
the back of FiDo—

everyone laughed like

CRaZy!

And then to top it all off,
Blockhead **barked**!

WOOF WOOF!

The crowd went **wild!**

After we'd run one lap,
the crowd asked for **MORE!**

MORE!   MORE!

MORE!

MORE!

So we ran around **again**!

And **again!**

WOOF WOOF!

Henry laughed <u>**so**</u> **much** that his popper juice ➤ shot out his <u>nose!</u>

FiDo and **Blockhead** were the

STARS

of the

SHOW !

'Quick,' said Granddad. 'Film them, Weir!'

I turned on the camera
just in time!

Everyone in our family loves hanging out with our pets.

Blockhead and Dad sometimes **dance together.**

electric boogaloo

Roger and FiDo love **crawling** under **things** together.

Blockhead, Mum and Sally sometimes have **sing-a-longs**.

And I <u>really love</u> taking FiDo for **walks**.

We like walking to the park near our house and playing a game where we **COPY each other**.

When FiDo **rolls over**, I roll over.

When FiDo **pokes his _tongue_ out**, I poke
my tongue out.

When FiDo **lies back and sticks his legs
in the air**, I lie back and stick my legs in the air.

Just then, I heard a voice . . .

It was **Bella**!

Bella was playing frisbee with Tiny and asked if
we wanted to join in.

Of course we did!

It was <u>SO</u> MUCH FUN!

We threw the **frisbee**

all around

the park!

But then I threw the frisbee **way too high** and it flew into a tree.

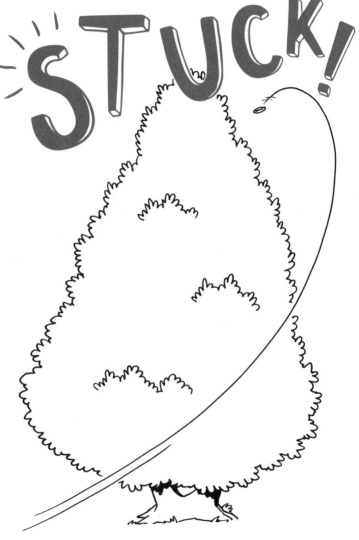

'Oops, sorry, Bella,' I said. 'You wait here. I'll climb up and get it.'

So I climbed until I couldn't climb any further and I reached as high as I could!

But I just

couldn't

reach it!

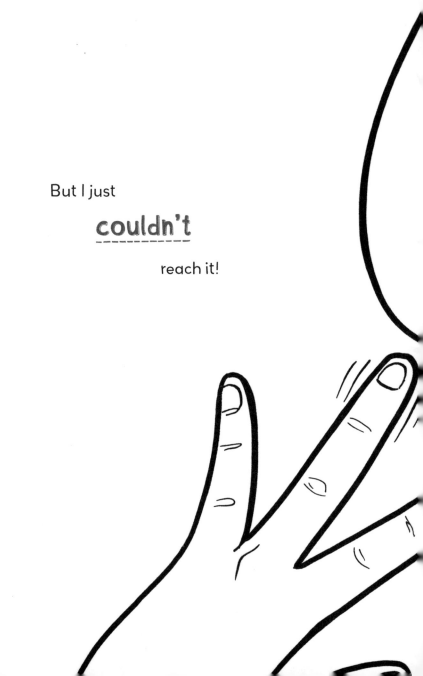

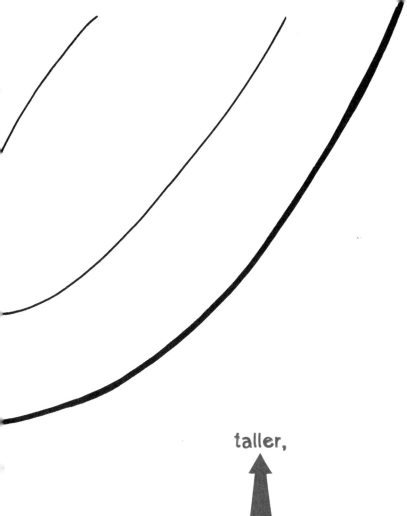

taller,

If only I was a **little bit** I would have been able to get the frisbee back for Bella.

SORRY, BELLA

'That's okay, Weir,' said Bella. 'I'll go get my Dad and he'll be able to reach it.'

I was **SOOO** embarrassed.

That night at dinner, I was telling Mum and Dad how I wished I was taller.

'That's alright,' said Dad, 'you're still growing.'

'Yeah, but I'll never be **really** tall,' I said.
'If I was taller, I'd be great at basketball.'

'You might not be great at basketball, Weir,
but you're **really great at other things**,'
said Mum. 'Like ... **drawing**!'

It was true, I **could** draw.

A

B Fold line B over to meet line A

'Yeah,' said Granddad. 'And you're really good at **filming things**, too.'

'That video you took of Blockhead and FiDo on Pet Day is **really <u>cool</u>**,' said Sally. 'Who knows, Weir, maybe one day you'll end up being a **famous movie director!**

<u>Imagine that!</u>'

YES. YOU'RE RIGHT.
TOY STORY 6
IS MY BEST MOVIE
SO FAR.

WEIR DO

Just then, I came up with a **great idea**!

LET'S SEND
THE VIDEO OF FIDO
AND BLOCKHEAD
TO FUNNIEST PETS!

How cool would it be if they were watching their **favourite TV show** together ... and then saw themselves on it!?

YEAH! AWESOME! LET'S DO IT!

So Granddad and Sally helped me send in
the video.

We could **hardly wait** for the next episode of

FiDo and Blockhead were **SOOO excited** to watch it, and they had **NO IDEA** that we'd sent **their video** to the show!

COMING UP NEXT. **FUNNIEST PETS!**

'Do you think they'll show the video of FiDo and Blockhead?' I asked Dad.

'Let's watch and find out!' said Dad.

As usual, the show was **HILARIOUS!**

There was a **piglet** in mud wearing gumboots.

There was a **kitten** falling asleep on a piano...

and then   waking herself up
                        accidentally!

And a video of a **hamster** in a tiny hammock, wearing sunglasses.

But <u>no</u> **Fido** and <u>no</u> **Blockhead** ...

'Maybe they'll be on next week's show,' said Sally.

'Yeah, maybe,' I said.

All of a sudden, FiDo and Blockhead both started **barking**!

STAY TUNED,
WE'VE SAVED THE BEST
FOR LAST . . .

HEY,
COOL!

ONE OF OUR HOME VIEWERS—
A KID CALLED <u>WEIRDO</u>—
SENT US THIS <u>AWESOME</u> VIDEO
OF HIS PETS,
FIDO AND BLOCKHEAD!

We couldn't believe it! FiDo and Blockhead

WERE ON TV!

CHAPTER 5

In the morning, we woke to <u>LOUD</u> banging on the front door.

BANG! BANG!

BANG!

'Weir, could you please get it?' said Mum. 'My hair looks **funny** again.'

The banging on the front door kept going.

bed hair

BANG!

BANG!

I climbed out of bed and wandered to the door.

I **couldn't _believe_** what I found there!

'What's going on?'
I asked Henry.

'The video!' he said.

'The video?'

'The video of FiDo and Blockhead on **Funniest Pets**!' said Henry. 'The TV show! **Everyone saw it!** You're famous!'

FAMOUS?

WHERE'S FIDO?
WHERE'S BLOCKHEAD?
WE WANT TO SEE THEM!

'Uh, I don't know,' I said. 'I just woke up—'

'There they are!' everyone shouted.

Suddenly, **FiDo** poked his head out of the door and **Blockhead** landed on my shoulder.

The crowd went **nuts**, calling to them and rushing towards us to get a **better look**.

CAMERAS FLASHED.

And flashed.

And flashed.

There was a loud

SQUAWK!

beside me as Blockhead **panicked**.

Oh no.

'Please stop,' I called out. 'Blockhead doesn't like flashing lights!'

But it was <u>too late</u>...

He'd flown away into the sky, far far away from the flashing cameras . . . and

far

far

away

from home!

CHAPTER 6

We **searched** <u>all day</u> for Blockhead, but couldn't find him **anywhere**!

BLOCKHEAD!
BLOCKHEAD!
WHERE <u>ARE</u> YOU?

Henry and **Mo** joined in.

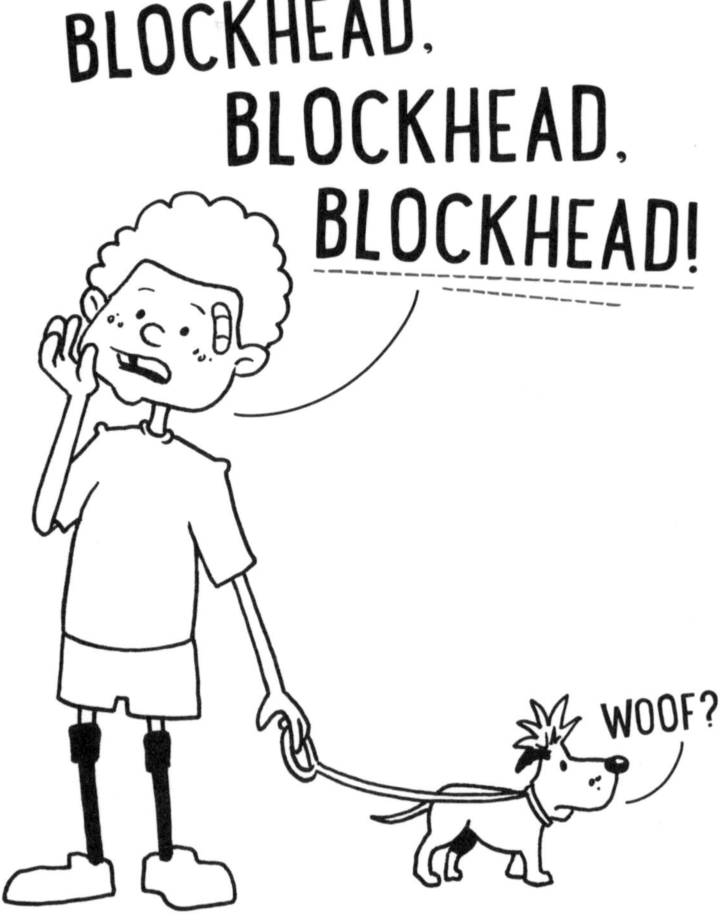

Bella and Tiny, too.

AROOOOOO!

BLOCKHEAD!
BLOCKHEAD!

We looked in **all of his _favourite_ places**.

We checked the **creek** where we sometimes take him for a bird bath.

We checked the **bird shop** where we buy his birdseed.

We even checked the **TV shop** where Blockhead and FiDo sometimes like to watch TV.

Sally and Henry helped me put up some
missing posters.

LOST BIRD

Answers to Blockhead, Blockie and Hey Bird!

LIKES: Wriggling, mooing, barking. Most of all, likes playing with his best friend, FiDo.

DOESN'T LIKE: Flashing lights.

REWARD: Anything you like from Henry's pet rock collection.

I was **really worried** about Blockhead. I could tell FiDo was, too. He kept **wuff-wuffing**, calling out to his friend.

WUFF?
WUFF?

'It'll be okay,' said Bella. 'You'll find him.'

'I hope so,' I replied.

'Woof!' said Tiny.

Then he gave me and FiDo

a **HUGE** lick.

UMM, THANKS, TINY

We were all making
our way back home
when Dad got a
phone call.

I got a **little bit <u>excited</u>**. Maybe someone
had found Blockhead!

'It was the Fire Crew,' said Dad. 'Sounds like there might be a dog stuck in the old shed at school. They've asked me if I can go and check it out.'

OH . . .

'Hey, Weir,' said Dad, 'why don't you and FiDo come with me?'

UMM . . .

'Come on,' said Dad, 'we'll keep a lookout for Blockhead on the way.'

It was **exciting** being on a __real-life__ **firefighting** job with Dad ... except that

there was **no fire** ...

and **Blockhead** was still missing ...

and **I was at school** . . .

on the __WEEKEND!__

A few people were standing around, waiting for us near the school gate.

'The barking was coming from over there,' one lady said, pointing to the shed.

'Who knows how a dog got in there,' said another guy, 'but I'm sure he would like to get back out!'

'**Absolutely**,' said Dad. 'Come on, Weir and FiDo. **Let's go**.'

CHAPTER 7

Dad unbolted the shed and we took a look inside.

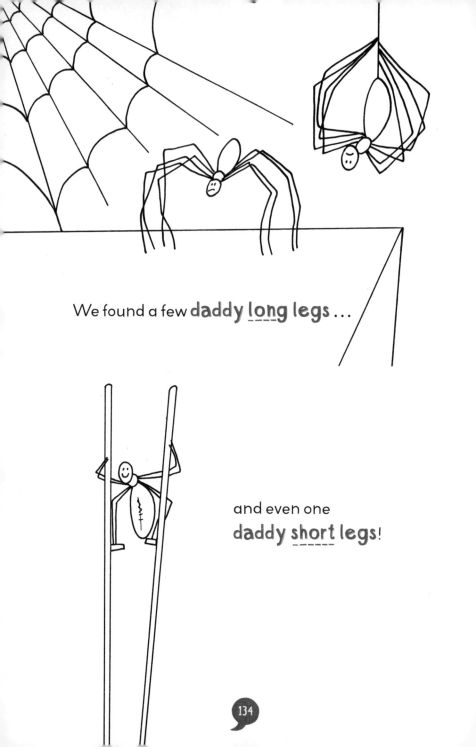

We found a few **daddy long legs** ...

and even one
daddy short legs!

But there was **no sign of a dog**!

We were thinking he must have found a
way out, when we heard **barking**!

We looked inside again ... but there was
definitely no dog in there!

Just the spiders!

WOOF

WOOF

We'd just about
**run out of
ideas**, when we
realised FiDo had
wandered off.

We found him
wriggling
behind the back
of the shed.

FiDo

138

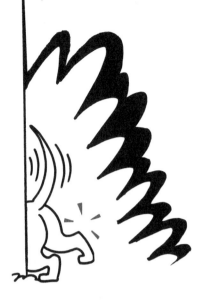

'FiDo, come back, boy,' called Dad.

But FiDo **wriggled in further.**

'FiDo,' I called.

But he'd **already disappeared** behind the shed.

WUFF! WUFF! WUFF!

'What is it, FiDo?' I called out. 'What have you found back there?'

Dad tried to follow him . . .

He **tried**...

and **tried**...

... and tried!

But no amount of **wriggling** was going to **squeeze** him through!

I suddenly realised that **I could fit** through!

'Dad, can I have a go?' I asked.

'Sure thing, Weir!'

Dad stepped out of the way
and I began **wriggling**
behind the shed.

Wriggling behind the shed
was **easy for me**...
I guess
being small
    helps sometimes!

It was **Blockhead** who was **barking** all along!

lockhead had hurt his wing flying behind the school shed, but he's <u>**much better**</u> already.

<u>**Everyone's**</u> been helping him rest up.

Tiny

Mo

CHAPTER 8

Especially me and FiDo.

Dad thinks I'll make an **awesome** firefighter one day. And maybe even FiDo could join me as a **rescue** dog.

For Summer Do
the 4th
little Weirdo!

FROM ANH

ACKNOWLEDGEMENTS

FROM JULES

For my Mum and Dad,
who encouraged me to be
anything I wanted,
as long as I gave it my best.

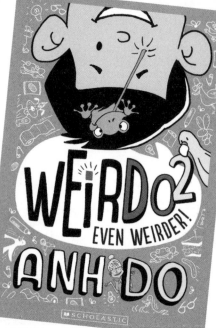

STAY
TUNED!